Iris and Walter
and Cousin Howie

Iris and Walter

and Cousin Howie

WRITTEN BY

Elissa Haden Guest

ILLUSTRATED BY

Christine Davenier

GULLIVER BOOKS

HARCOURT, INC.

ORLANDO   AUSTIN   NEW YORK

SAN DIEGO   TORONTO   LONDON

For my husband, Nick—E. H. G.

For my dear cousin, Sylvie Toux—C. D.

Text copyright © 2003 by Elissa Haden Guest
Illustrations copyright © 2003 by Christine Davenier

www.HarcourtBooks.com

Gulliver Books is a trademark of Harcourt, Inc.,
registered in the United States of America and/or other jurisdictions.

Library of Congress Cataloging-in-Publication Data
Guest, Elissa Haden.
Iris and Walter and Cousin Howie/written by Elissa Haden Guest;
illustrated by Christine Davenier.
p.   cm.
"Gulliver Books."
Summary: Walter's favorite cousin is coming to visit, but Iris is disappointed
when Howie does not turn out to be so great—or friendly—after all.
[1. Cousins—Fiction.   2. Friendship—Fiction.]   I. Davenier, Christine, ill.
II. Title.   III. Series: Guest, Elissa Haden. Iris and Walter; bk. 6.
PZ7.G9375Isk   2003
[E]—dc21   2002012394
ISBN 0-15-216695-5

First edition
H G F E D C B A
Manufactured in China

Contents

1. Walter's Great News

One day, Iris and Baby Rose
were playing in the sunshine
when Iris's best friend, Walter,
came running up the path.
"Iris, I have great news!"
he shouted. "My cousin
Howie is coming to visit
this weekend."

"Howie, the one who knows magic tricks?"
asked Iris.
"That's the one," said Walter.
"I can't wait for you to meet him."

"Me, too," said Iris. "Do you think
Howie can teach me magic tricks?"
"Why not!" said Walter.

That night at supper, Iris told
her family about Cousin Howie.

"He's nine years old,
and he's Walter's favorite cousin.
Howie taught Walter how to fish, and
he's going to teach *me* magic tricks."

"I might be a magician
when I grow up," said Iris.
"A magician!" said her father.
"Goodness me!" said her mother.
"How delightful," said Grandpa.

Every day after school, Iris and Walter talked about Howie's visit.

"We can show him our tree house," said Walter.

"We can take turns riding Rain," said Iris.

Walter couldn't wait for his best friend
and his favorite cousin to meet.
"The three of us are going to have
so much fun," said Walter.

2. Cousin Howie

Saturday morning, Iris hopped on her bike
and rode over to Walter's house.
Walter and Howie were sitting in Walter's
hammock. They were laughing and talking.
Howie was sitting where Iris always sat.

"Iris, this is my cousin Howie," said Walter.
"Hello," said Iris.
"Hello," said Howie.

"Look at the fishing pole Howie gave me,"
said Walter.
"It used to be mine," said Howie.
"I caught a lot of fish with it."
Iris picked up the fishing pole.
"You're holding it wrong," said Howie.

Iris pretended she was fishing.
"Careful. Don't break it," said Howie.
"I *won't*," said Iris.
She handed the pole back to Walter.

"Isn't it great?" asked Walter.
Iris didn't see what was so great
about an old fishing pole.
But Walter thought it was wonderful.

That night, Iris's father asked,
"So, how was the famous Cousin Howie?"
"He's kind of bossy," said Iris.
"He is?" asked her father.
"Yes," said Iris. "I don't think he's very
friendly."

"Maybe Howie is shy," said Iris's mother. "Maybe he just needs a little time to warm up." But Iris was not so sure.

3. Fishing Troubles

The next morning, Iris put on her cape.
"Why, Iris, look at you," said her mother.
"You look *just* like a magician,"
said her father.
"I'm going to ask Howie to teach me some
magic tricks," said Iris, and off she rode.

"Oh, Iris, honey, the boys aren't here,"
said Walter's mother. "They went fishing."
"Oh," said Iris.

Iris rode over to the pond.
Walter and Howie were fishing
from the big rock.
It was very quiet.

"Hi, everybody!" Iris shouted.
"*Ssh!*" said Howie. "You'll scare away
the fish."

"Catch anything yet?" she asked.
"Not yet," said Walter.
"How long does it take
to catch a fish?" asked Iris.
"It's hard to know," said Howie.

"Hey, Howie, Walter says you know
magic tricks. Can you teach me some?"
asked Iris. "Do you say 'ABRACADABRA'?"
she cried.

"*Iris,* we're never going to catch anything if you keep scaring the fish," said Howie. "Does she have to do *everything* with us?" he whispered to Walter. But Iris heard.

"I just remembered
I have to go home," said Iris.
Iris rode home as fast as she could.

"Back so soon?" asked Iris's mother.
Iris burst into tears.

4. A Little Magic

"I hate that Cousin Howie," Iris sobbed.
When Baby Rose saw her big sister
crying, she started to cry, too.
"Oh, dear, it's a house full of tears,"
said Iris's mother. "Iris, my love, tell me
what happened."

Iris told her mother all about Cousin Howie.
"Howie's *mean*," said Iris.
"I can see how he hurt your feelings, my Iris,"
said Iris's mother. "It sounds like he wanted
Walter all to himself."

"Walter's *my* best friend!" Iris told her father.
"Of course he is," said Iris's father.
"And you're *Walter's* best friend.
Cousin Howie isn't going to change that."

"I don't like Howie!" Iris told Grandpa.
"Iris, my girl, you don't
have to like him," said Grandpa.

"And I think fishing is boring!" said Iris.
"So do I," whispered Grandpa.

Grandpa gave Iris his handkerchief.
It was clean and soft,
and it smelled like Grandpa.
"I didn't even learn any magic tricks,"
Iris sniffed.

"But, Iris, you don't need Howie
to learn magic tricks," said Grandpa.
"We can go to the library.
I'm sure we'll find a book about magic."

Early the next morning, Iris woke up
to the *clop, clop, clop* of horse hooves.
She raced outside.

"Hello, Iris," said Walter.
"Hi, Walter," said Iris.

"I'm sorry Howie wasn't very friendly,
and I'm sorry he didn't teach you any
magic tricks," said Walter.
"But, Walter, we can learn
our own magic tricks," said Iris.

Iris showed Walter her library book.
"Wow," said Walter. "Do you want to put on
a magic show?"
"Sure!" said Iris.
"We'll have to practice a lot," said Walter.
"Some of these tricks look really, really hard."

But for magicians like Iris and Walter,
anything was possible.

The illustrations in this book were created in pen-and-ink on keacolor paper.
The display type was set in Elroy.
The text type was set in Fairfield Medium.
Color separations by Colourscan Co. Pte. Ltd., Singapore
Manufactured by South China Printing Company, Ltd., China
This book was printed on totally chlorine-free Enso Stora Matte paper.
Production supervision by Sandra Grebenar and Wendi Taylor
Designed by Lydia D'moch and Suzanne Fridley